PETE RAMSEY and the John Thing

by Bonnie Highsmith Taylor

Cover Illustration: Dea Marks
Inside Illustration: Dea Marks

For: Lisa Miller
Brian McCown
Janet Reddington
Char Jones
Danny Highsmith, Jr.
Jennifer McCown

© 2001 Perfection Learning®
First ebook edition 2012
www.perfectionlearning.com

10 11 12 13 14 15 QG 17 16 15 14 13 12

55787
PB ISBN: 978-0-7891-2380-0
RLB ISBN: 978-0-7807-7743-9
eISBN: 978-1-6138-4976-7

Printed in the United States of America

400583632

CONTENTS

1

Toilet Noises

Pete Ramsey woke up early Wednesday morning. He decided that he was *not* going to school.

It was "Take Care of Your Teeth Week" or some such thing. And the class was putting on a play. Pete wasn't about to be a tooth in a silly play. Being a tooth was bad enough. But a rotten tooth? No way!

A lot of kids had to be teeth. But at least they were white, shiny, healthy teeth. Pete's best friend, Arthur Robinson, was Dr. Brushright, the dentist. Arthur got to jab Pete with a dental tool while Pete yelled, "Ooh! Oh! Ow!"

Samantha Day was the prettiest girl in the whole school. She was Miss Sparkle, the dental assistant in the play.

Only Miss Ryan would make a sixth-grade class do a play for first graders. That was because Miss Ryan used to be a first-grade teacher.

Pete decided to try the stomachache act. Sometimes it worked. Sometimes it didn't.

He let Mom call for him twice without answering her.

"Pete, time to get up!" his mom yelled. "Pete, did you hear me?"

Finally Pete's mom opened his bedroom door. Pete was curled into a tight ball. He was groaning loudly.

"Stomachache, huh?" said Mom.

Pete groaned louder.

"I hope it's not appendicitis," Mom said in that cool voice that made Pete mad. "Or your gall bladder. You're so young to have surgery."

Pete screwed up his face. "Oh, it's not that, Mom," he panted. "It's just a bad stomachache. Probably from those carrots you made me eat last night." He took a couple of short breaths. "I-I was afraid this would happen. But-but I ate them to please you."

"Good boy," Mom said. Then she felt his forehead. "I'll write a note to Miss Ryan. I'll tell her to rush you to the hospital if you have any pain."

"But, Mom . . . ," Pete moaned.

"Don't worry," Mom said calmly. "I'll be there in time for the operation."

"But, Mom . . . ," Pete moaned.

"Up!" Mom said.

"But—" Pete began.

"Up! Up! Up!" Mom repeated.

It hadn't worked.

Pete got up and got dressed. Then he walked into the kitchen. Mom had told Dad everything. Pete could tell by the look on Dad's face.

They had bacon and pancakes for breakfast. Pete tried to act sick. But he couldn't keep from gulping down the food.

Dad sat across the table. He was grinning that awful grin that made Pete fume.

"Isn't this the day of the play?" asked Mom. "The play you said you'd rather die than be in?"

Dad burst out laughing.

"Well—well—how would you like to be a rotten tooth?" Pete sputtered angrily.

Pete jumped up, nearly knocking his chair over. He stormed out the back door. He didn't see the skateboard at the foot of the steps until it was too late. And then he was gliding straight for the apple tree—head-on.

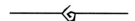

An hour later, Pete lay on a table in the doctor's office.

"A slight sprain of the ankle," said Dr. Quenton. "And a slight scrape on the forehead." He pulled Pete's eyelids out and shined a light in his eyes. "And possibly a slight concussion. Very, very slight. Watch for signs."

"What kinds of signs?" Mom asked.

"Dilated pupils and vomiting," said Dr. Quenton. "Keep him quiet for a day or two."

Everything was only *slight*. And Pete felt his parents were only *slightly* concerned. They were too busy arguing about missing work.

Mom solved the argument. "There's no way I can stay home today," she said. "I'm showing a house to a possible buyer at two o'clock. I have to be there."

Darn, thought Pete. There goes any sympathy I might have gotten.

Dad went to the drugstore. He got some stuff the doctor had suggested. Pete was supposed to soak his ankle in it.

"Epsom salts," Dr. Quenton had called it. "It's an old-fashioned cure. But it's better than some of the newfangled things on the market."

Dr. Quenton was old-fashioned himself. And old, thought Pete. He was at least fifty.

Pete was lying in bed. He had an ice bag on his head. And his foot was propped up on a pillow.

Pete wished his friend Arthur were here right now. For a boy, Arthur was very kind.

Once in a while, Dad made a crack about Arthur. Like he thought Arthur was a sissy. But Pete knew better.

Sure, Arthur was always spotlessly clean, neatly dressed, and polite. But he was a regular guy. Arthur was the brain of the class. And he usually had his nose in a book.

You'd never know it to look at Arthur, but he was great at sports. He played scientifically. That's the way he did everything.

Pete raised the ice bag and tried to blink his eyes. They felt funny. He wondered if they were dilated.

Actually, a slight concussion didn't sound all that bad to Pete. He didn't like the idea of vomiting. But the dilated pupils might be cool. It was sure to make a guy look pitiful.

Pete heard Dad open and close the front door. Pete was looking forward to sitting in front of the TV. Just soaking his ankle in a pan of warm water and eating snacks.

But Dad's footsteps passed Pete's room. A moment later, Pete heard water running in the bathtub.

The next thing Pete knew, Dad had pulled off his pajamas. Then Dad scooped Pete up in his arms and carried him to the bathroom. He placed him in a tub of hot water. The tub was slippery from the Epsom salts.

"There," Dad said.

"There what?" asked Pete.

"There—soak," said Dad.

"But, Dad," Pete said. "The doctor didn't say to soak my whole body."

"It sure can't hurt," said Dad. "Besides, I don't think we have a pan big enough for your foot."

With that, Dad left the room and shut the door.

Pete scrunched down in the tub. "It would serve him right if I caught pneumonia," he grumbled.

Pete wondered if kids were missing him at school. Arthur would miss him, of course. And Yibbet might.

Yibbet was a girl. But not a regular girl. The guys forgot most of the time that she was a girl at all. She could out-arm wrestle any boy in school—except Arthur. He arm wrestled scientifically. So it was a battle of wits against strength. And Arthur was smarter than Yibbet was strong.

Yibbet's actual name was Elizabeth Dixon. But Bobzee, her little brother Robert Zachary, couldn't say "Elizabeth." The closest he came was "Yibbet." And the name stuck.

Pete was pretty sure Yibbet would miss him. But it was Samantha who really counted. He could pretend she would miss him. And that she would feel bad about what had happened to him.

Mom had stopped at school. She had told Miss Ryan why Pete wouldn't be there.

Pete's thoughts were interrupted by a noise. It seemed to be coming from the toilet. A splashing noise. He sat up straight and peered over the edge of the tub. The toilet lid was down. But water was oozing from underneath it and running on the floor.

The splashing really got loud.

"Hey, Dad!" Pete yelled.

"Not yet," Dad called back. "Sit there and soak."

"But, Dad," Pete yelled. "There's something strange going on in the toilet."

"Like what?" roared Dad.

"Like—uh—like a fish or something splashing around," Pete said.

Pete could hear Dad's deep chuckle. It drifted under the bathroom door.

"Aw, nuts!" Pete mumbled as the splashing continued.

Pete worked his good leg up under his body. Then he pulled himself over the edge of the tub. He hopped to the toilet. He slowly slipped his fingers under the lid and threw it back, banging the tank hard.

The waves, dashing over the rim, splattered against Pete's leg. Wide-eyed and breathless, Pete watched as the waves gradually stopped. The toilet water calmed to a smooth surface.

Pete shook his head and blinked his eyes. Then he fell to his knees and froze.

2

Sewer Suspicions

Pete blinked when Dad opened the bathroom door.
Dad was carrying a towel and Pete's pajamas.

Pete was still on his knees, shaking all over.

"What are you doing out of the tub?" Dad asked.
"How long did you soak?"

Pete tried to speak, but nothing came out.

"Hey, Pete," Dad said, puzzled. "What's wrong? Are
you okay?"

Pete's jaw was quivering, only partly from being
wet and cold. "I'm f-f-fine," he stuttered.

Pete kept an eye on the toilet as Dad helped him into his pajamas. Then Dad carried him back to bed. Dad tucked the covers under Pete's chin. Pete felt his father's eyes studying him.

Why didn't he just tell Dad what he'd seen? thought Pete. Why didn't he tell Dad how the water splashed right out of the toilet? Like something was in there swimming around. Because Dad would laugh his head off, that's why.

Dad ran his fingers through Pete's hair. He never did that. "Are you sure you're okay, fella?" he asked. Dad was staring at him strangely.

Pete nodded.

Dad edged toward the door. "I-I guess you'd better get some rest," he said.

As soon as Dad left, Pete threw back the covers and sat up in bed. His legs were still trembling. They felt like rubber hoses. But he managed to hop over to the dresser and look in the mirror.

Pete flinched. No wonder Dad had stared at him. Pete's face was white. The freckles across his nose and cheeks looked like ink spots. And his eyes—well—if they weren't dilating, they were sure doing something. They looked like they were ready to pop out of his head and roll across the floor.

Pete hopped back into bed. He tried to make some sense out of what had happened. Or what he *thought* had happened.

That was it! He had only *thought* it had happened. Maybe he had even dozed off for a minute in the warm water and dreamed it. Or maybe the concussion had made his mind do crazy things.

Pete lay in bed thinking about what he *thought* had happened. Then he finally went to sleep.

At noon, Dad brought Pete a bowl of soup and a sandwich.

Later, Dad came back for the tray. "You-you be sure to yell if you need anything," he told Pete.

But Pete had a strange feeling. Like Dad was hoping he *didn't* need anything. Dad was still looking at Pete as though he didn't know him.

Later, Arthur stopped by on his way home from school. Pete was really glad to see him.

"Uh—did anybody miss me a little?" Pete asked.

"Oh, yes," said Arthur. "All of your friends missed you. Ted, Evan, Brad, and, of course, me. Yibbet mentioned your absence several times." He paused for a moment, thinking. "And Samantha expressed deep concern over your unfortunate accident."

Pete's heart skipped a couple of beats. Samantha *had* missed him!

"I do believe, though," Arthur said, "that Dwight Phillips missed you most of all."

"Dwight Phillips!" Pete said. "I barely know him. How come *he* missed me?"

Arthur grinned. "Dwight had to take your part in the play," he said.

Pete was enjoying his friend's company. But he couldn't seem to keep his mind off what had happened. Or what he *thought* had happened. He was almost sure Arthur wouldn't laugh. So Pete decided to tell him.

When Pete finished the story, Arthur very flatly stated, "Most interesting."

"Yeah," Pete agreed. "A concussion can make things really kooky."

Arthur studied his friend's face. "I've seen concussions before," he said. "A boy at camp got hit in the head with a bat. And my uncle was in an automobile accident. The pupils are quite dilated in a concussion. But, Pete, your eyes look the same as always."

Pete tried to giggle. "Suppose—just suppose—that it really did happen," he said. "What would be a good reason?"

"This is an older house," Arthur said. "The plumbing could be needing repairs. Maybe they're working on a sewer line somewhere in the neighborhood. I suppose air bubbles working into the pipes could cause it."

After Arthur went home, Pete thought it over. Arthur's thoughts made sense. And he felt a little better knowing he probably wasn't going bonkers.

Mom brought Pete hot chocolate that evening. She read to him while he drank it.

Pete loved to have Mom read to him. After a couple of chapters, she started to leave. But then she stopped. "What's this I hear about a fish?" she asked. "Or something splashing around in the toilet?"

Pete sucked in his breath and swallowed. "N-nothing, Mom," Pete said. "Uh—I was just playing a joke on Dad."

His mother gave him a shame-on-you look. Then she closed the door behind her.

Just before Pete dozed off, he heard Mom talking to Dad. "I see what you mean," she said. "He *is* acting a little strange. I'll stay home tomorrow."

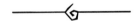

Pete's ankle was much better the next morning. He could put some weight on it. He felt pretty good. So Mom didn't think he had to stay in bed all day.

"But I'm warning you," Mom said. "I'm going to clean house. So stay out of my way or into bed you'll go."

Pete promised.

Mom spent the morning cleaning. She seemed to be having the time of her life. She danced through the house as she vacuumed, scrubbed, and dusted. She sang at the top of her lungs.

Pete had a plan. But until Mom settled down somewhere for a while, he couldn't try it.

Pete wanted to check all the plumbing in the house. Including the old laundry tubs in the basement. Mom had never washed clothes in the basement. It was too dark and cold down there. Dad had closed in the large back porch for a utility room.

Maybe, Pete thought, the old pipes are rusty or plugged. Arthur might be right. That could be the problem.

But Pete had a hard time checking things out. Mom was everywhere. Once, he tried to get into the bathroom and almost fell over her. She was on her knees scrubbing the toilet bowl.

Why didn't it happen now? Pete wondered. It would scare Mom out of her wits. But at least then they'd believe him.

"Pete," Mom said after lunch, "I want you to go to your room and rest. I'm going to sew for a while."

Good, thought Pete. But he didn't plan to rest. At least not yet.

Pete started with the basement. He turned on both faucets full blast and filled the laundry tubs. Then he pulled the plugs and hobbled up to the bathroom as fast as he could.

The water in the toilet bowl remained calm. He flushed the toilet. Nothing. He flushed it again and again. He sat on the edge of the tub staring into the toilet for over an hour. Nothing.

"Looks like you're well enough to go back to school tomorrow, Pete," Dad said at dinner.

Pete nodded.

"Good," said Mom. "I'm showing the Westmark house tomorrow. It's a big, old mansion. What a great sale that would be!"

Pete got an idea. "Hey, Mom," he said. "What if you wanted to sell this house? Would it be hard to do?"

Mom looked puzzled. "Why would it be?" she asked.

"Well, it's pretty old," Pete said. "The wiring is probably worn out. And the plumbing must be getting bad."

"It may be old, but it's in good shape," Dad said. "We had it rewired five years ago. And the pipes were all checked last spring after that bad freeze. The plumbing is in tip-top shape."

"I wouldn't be too sure," Mom said. She sounded like she was trying to keep from smiling. "I could swear I heard water running half the afternoon. And the toilet must have flushed at least a dozen times—all by itself."

Pete didn't look up. But he knew their eyes were glued to his face.

3

A Voice in the Toilet

Pete was actually glad to get back to school. Especially when Samantha said, "I think it's so terrible about your accident, Peter."

Pete's ankle was fine now. But he didn't think it would hurt to limp just a little bit.

Pete talked to Arthur before class.

"You seemed so upset about that toilet incident," said Arthur. "So I took the time to check around the neighborhood. As far as I could tell, there was nothing going on. I'm inclined to think it's due to faulty plumbing somewhere in the house itself."

Pete started to tell Arthur that the plumbing was fine. But he decided against it. It wasn't important anymore. Pete had made up his mind. It was just one of those weird things that happen sometimes. And it would never happen again. Never. He was sure of it.

Right now, Pete's mind was on Samantha. Pete had two days' worth of milk money. He was sure Mom would forget about it. With that money and his allowance, he could treat Samantha to an ice cream bar after lunch.

Pete and Arthur walked into the classroom and sat down. Then Pete found out what the assignment was while he'd been absent. He was glad he had missed those two days!

It was poetry! Not just reading it. But *writing* it!

Pete started to breathe a sigh of relief. But Miss Ryan said, "Peter, I know you haven't had time to prepare. But try to write something while the others are reading their poems. Something that expresses an emotion."

Oh, yuck! Miss Ryan and her thing about self-expression!

Pete struggled with a poem. And he thought about when Miss Ryan had been his first-grade teacher. She was *really* into that self-expression stuff then.

Miss Ryan would have the class express themselves in art. Painting, drawing, and modeling. Pete always chose modeling. He liked the feel of the gooey clay.

Once, he had rolled his clay into a big, round ball. Then he had stuck his finger into it about fifty times. Miss Ryan studied Pete and his creation for a long time.

"This is good, Peter," Miss Ryan had said. "You have a deep mind."

It was still on a shelf in Pete's bedroom. He had even made a nameplate for his masterpiece. He called it "Ball of Clay with Holes Poked in It."

Dad had gotten a real bang out of it.

Usually, Arthur helped Pete with assignments like this. But now Pete was on his own.

Pete looked up from his blank paper. It was Samantha's turn to read her poem.

Samantha always began with a nod of her head. Then she gave a cute little smile before she began.

"The subject of my poem is love," Samantha said. "My love is deep, my love is true. My love is strong, my love is you."

Pete's heart fluttered. She means *me!* he thought wildly.

"That's very good, Samantha," said Miss Ryan.

Samantha nodded shyly. Her skirt brushed Pete's arm as she walked past his desk. Pete felt instant goose pimples.

Brad was next. His poem was about thunder. Evan's was about war. Ted's was about spring. Beth's was about horses. Yibbet's was about tennis.

Pete thought Yibbet had made up some of the words. But Miss Ryan said it showed a lot of imagination.

Arthur, of course, held the class spellbound. Most likely because they didn't understand a thing he was talking about.

The title of his poem was "Soliloquy of a Sojourner." And it didn't rhyme at all. It was free verse, Miss Ryan explained. A most difficult form to master.

"Oh, my, Arthur!" Miss Ryan gushed. "You *do* have a way with words!"

Arthur has a way with words all right, thought Pete. A nutty way.

Suddenly, Miss Ryan's voice echoed in Pete's ears. "And now, Peter. Let's see what you've come up with."

Pete's face was bright red as he walked to the front on rubbery legs. He limped a little, for effect. In a squeaky voice, he announced the title of his poem.

"My Accident," Pete read. His voice conked out.

"Uh—" Pete swallowed. "I—"

"Just relax, Peter," said Miss Ryan. "Take a deep breath now."

Pete took a nice deep breath—a deep, deep breath. Then he blurted, "I bumped my head and went to bed."

Pete rushed to his seat as the class began laughing.

The laughter continued.

"I won't give you a grade until Monday, Peter," Miss Ryan finally said. "When you turn in something more—uh—suitable."

Lunch came at last. Pete sat with Arthur and the rest of his friends. He gulped down his sandwich and orange. He hoped he'd finish before Samantha did.

No one else was in line at the snack bar. Pete bought two chocolate fudge ice cream bars. Then he headed toward Samantha's table. She always sat with her girlfriends.

Halfway there, Pete stopped in his tracks. Samantha was not with her girlfriends. She was sitting with Dwight Phillips!

Pete whirled around and ran into Yibbet.

"Hi, Pete," said Yibbet.

"Hi," said Pete. Then he handed Yibbet an ice cream bar.

Pete slowly walked home after school. He took shortcuts through back alleys. He was grateful that it was Friday. He would have two days to get over his broken heart.

Pete had been so sure Samantha liked him. He thought she'd even meant the poem for him. And all the time it was Dwight Phillips. What could she possibly see in him? He was sort of good-looking and a little smart. But he wasn't even popular.

Pete hauled off and kicked a big rock with his bad foot. Right away, he wished he hadn't. He hopped on his other foot, howling loudly. He didn't hear his friend calling to him.

Arthur finally caught up with Pete. "What in the world are you so perturbed about?" Arthur asked.

"What's 'perturbed'?" asked Pete. "You and your fancy words. You've been yapping fancy words all day. If it hadn't been for your stupid poem, Miss Ryan might have liked mine!"

Pete's insults didn't bother Arthur. "You must admit, Pete, it wasn't much of a poem," Arthur said. "Brevity might well be the soul of wit, but after all—"

Pete's glare stopped Arthur in midsentence.

Pete couldn't tell Arthur the real reason he was so "perturbed"—or whatever. Girl problems were one thing Arthur wasn't up on. And the poem matter wasn't that important now.

"I am truly sorry about your embarrassing scene with Miss Ryan and the class," said Arthur. "If I'd thought you felt up to it, I'd have told you of the assignment. Perhaps even helped you. But you were acting very strangely, if you remember."

Pete shook his head and grinned. Good old Arthur. Pete could always count on his friendship. Arthur never got mad. Even when Pete was unreasonable.

Pete slapped his friend on the back. "How about stopping by my place?" he asked. "Mom and Dad won't be home for a while."

"Excellent idea," said Arthur.

After three peanut butter and jelly sandwiches, the boys went outside. They wanted to practice a little football passing.

Arthur was good at football. He had a way of putting a little twist on the ball that really made it sail. With a couple of fantastic jumps, Pete was able to catch Arthur's first two passes.

But the third pass was way above Pete's reach. Before his feet had returned to the ground, he heard a thump behind him. It was Yibbet catching the football. Her jump had outdistanced his by a foot!

"Great catch!" yelled Arthur.

"Yeah!" said Pete with surprise.

Yibbet's little brother, Bobzee, was with her. "I'd play ball with you guys. But I have to watch my little brother," Yibbet said.

"Aw," groaned Pete and Arthur at the same time.

"We could use you for some long passes," said Pete.

"Wish I could," Yibbet said. "But Mom's having a bridge party. And all the women chipped in five dollars for me. My job is to keep the brat out of the living room."

"I'm not a brat!" howled Bobzee. And then he kicked Yibbet in the shin.

Yibbet drew back her hand. It was aimed directly at Bobzee's bottom.

"I'll tell Mama!" Bobzee screamed.

Yibbet's hand dropped to her side. "Sorry, guys," she said.

"Doesn't seem fair," Pete said. "Why should *you* always get stuck taking care of that little monster?"

The next thing Pete knew, he was flat on his back. Bobzee was pounding him in the face. His fists felt like they belonged to Muhammad Ali instead of a four-year-old boy.

"Who's a monster?" Bobzee screamed in Pete's ear.

Pete tried to untangle Bobzee's legs. They were wrapped around Pete's neck like a vise. "Get this monster off me!" he bellowed.

Arthur finally came to Pete's aid. Grabbing Bobzee around the waist, he swung him around. Pete had to dodge Bobzee's weapons—his arms and legs.

"Put me down!" yowled Bobzee. "I'll tell Mama!"

Pete sprang to his feet and scrambled a safe distance away. He couldn't believe his ears when Arthur said, "Promise to be a good boy, Bobzee. And Yibbet and Pete will apologize to you."

"Apologize!" exclaimed Pete. "Apologize for what? For not letting him kill me?"

"For calling him bad names," Arthur said. He set Bobzee on the ground and patted his head. "Nobody likes to be called names. He's not a monster or a brat. He's a nice little boy. Right, Bobzee?"

"I'm not a monster or a brat," repeated Bobzee. He smiled a sweet, sickening smile. "I'm a nice little boy." He paused, then quickly changed it to, "I'm a nice *big* boy."

Pete was all set to jump Arthur. But he caught Arthur's look just in time. It was the play-along-with-me look.

"That's right, Bobzee," Arthur said. Then he patted Bobzee's head some more. "You're a nice *big* boy. Now, Yibbet and Pete, tell Bobzee how sorry you are for calling him names."

Yibbet made a face. But she said, "Sorry, Bobzee," as though she were used to it.

Pete knew he would choke on the words. He just *knew* he would. His face was still stinging from the blows the "nice big boy" had dished out.

"Pete?" said Arthur.

A Voice in the Toilet

"I—I'm sorry you're a little monster," Pete began. "Uh—I mean—I'm sorry I called you a little monster."

Bobzee's smile stretched across his face. "I'm a nice *big* boy."

"You're a nice *big* boy," Pete said through his teeth.

"There now," Arthur said, rubbing his hands together. "Bobzee, will you be real, real nice and let Yibbet play ball with us? If Pete gives you some cookies and a glass of chocolate milk? And if he lets you sit in the house and watch television?"

The child's eyes sparkled. With lips stuck out at least three inches, Bobzee ran to his sister. He smacked noisily for a kiss.

Yibbet knelt down and gave her brother a quick kiss on his puckered mouth. "That's a good boy, Bobzee," Yibbet said.

"A good *big* boy," Bobzee reminded.

"Okay, Bobzee," Yibbet said as she flashed a fake smile. "A good *big* boy. Now run along while sister plays ball."

Like a small tornado, Bobzee whizzed toward the house. Pete was at his heels, grumbling all the way.

Pete fixed Bobzee a glass of chocolate milk and handed him three oatmeal cookies. Then he left Bobzee sitting in front of the TV set.

For the next hour, Pete, Yibbet, and Arthur had a great time. Yibbet could out-pass, out-catch, and out-jump both boys. But neither of them disliked her because of it. Yibbet was one of the guys.

Too bad, thought Pete, that Yibbet had to be born a girl. She'd have had a real future in football. Or just about any sport, for that matter.

"I don't know about you guys," Arthur said at last, "but I've worked up a huge appetite. I'm going home for dinner."

"Same here," said Yibbet. "And Mom will be missing her dear pet."

"I'll get him for you," Pete said, heading for the front door.

Inside, the TV was blaring away. The picture was all green. Fingerprints were all over the screen. And it was sticky. But Bobzee was nowhere to be seen.

Pete went into the kitchen. The refrigerator door was standing wide open. A chair was overturned. And the empty cookie jar was on the floor. But Bobzee was still nowhere to be seen.

Just then, Pete heard a noise coming from the bathroom. A thumping sound and Bobzee's voice yelling. "Mean old thing!" Bobzee shouted angrily. "Mean, dumb old thing!"

Holding his breath and hoping against the worst, Pete opened the bathroom door. What a mess! The floor was flooded. The toilet bowl was overflowing with toilet paper. Bobzee was kicking the toilet, taking turns with both feet. And he was throwing piece after piece of tissue into the crammed bowl.

"What's going on?" Pete shouted, slipping and sliding on the wet floor.

Bobzee kept kicking and throwing. "Mean old thing threw water all over me," he shouted.

Pete picked Bobzee up by the arms and carried him into the hall. "Go on home, you little monster!" Pete roared. "Get out!"

Pete grabbed all the towels off the racks. Then he began sopping up the water on the floor.

"Oh, brother!" Pete groaned. "If Mom and Dad see this mess, I'll be grounded for a month! Maybe a year! Maybe for life!"

Pete couldn't flush all the paper down the toilet. It would have flooded all over the floor again. He'd have to take at least part of it out by hand.

So Pete scooted the wastebasket over to the toilet. Shuddering, he began the horrible task.

Well, Arthur had to be right. In spite of what Dad had said, Pete thought. The plumbing was bad.

Pete scooped out all the paper that he possibly could. Then he stood up and reached for the handle. But before he could push it down, a gurgling sound came from the bowl. And water shot over the rim.

In terror, Pete froze. Finally, a small, squeaky voice came from deep in the toilet. "Don't flush!" the voice cried out. "Don't flush! Oh, please don't flush!"

4

The John Thing

Pete's parents found Pete sitting on the edge of the
tub. He was staring into the toilet bowl.

"What on earth are you doing?" asked Mom from
the doorway.

Pete jumped at the sound of her voice.

"N-Nothing, Mom," Pete stammered. He was still
looking into the toilet. "Just sitting here."

"I can see that," Mom said. "But why? And what are
you staring at?"

"Uh—the water in the toilet," Pete said.

"Peter Ramsey!" Mom yelled. "If you start that toilet thing again!" But then she spoke a little softer. "Pete, why are you staring into the toilet?"

"Because I can't help it," Pete said.

"Try," Mom said. She stepped inside the bathroom. She slipped on the wet floor and grabbed for the towel rack. But she missed and fell flat on her bottom.

Pete jerked out of his trance.

Dad was grinning in the doorway. He was reaching out for Mom. But he was careful not to step on the wet floor.

"Let me help you, Mom," said Pete. He offered his hand.

From her position on the floor, Mom slapped at one hand and then the other. "What's all over the floor?" she screamed.

"Just water," Pete said quietly.

"I know it's water," Mom said. Using the edge of the tub and the clothes hamper, she made it to her feet. "How did it get all over the floor?"

Pete took a deep breath. "Uh—Bobzee was here," he said.

Mom screamed again. Dad dropped his hand and left. He was mumbling something about lack of responsibility.

A moment later, Dad screamed too. "What's wrong with the television?" he yelled. "And what's this sticky stuff all over the screen?"

"Bobzee was here," Pete mumbled again.

Mom slipped out of her shoes. She grabbed some towels and finished mopping up the floor. Then she spied the wastebasket filled with sopping toilet paper. She looked up at Pete. Her eyes were questioning him.

Pete opened his mouth to speak.

"I know," Mom sighed. "Bobzee was here."

While Mom's back was turned, Pete squeezed past her. He made it safely back to his room. But his shaky legs almost gave out before he got there. With shaking hands, he closed the door.

Pete flopped down on his bed breathing hard. He shook his head. If he could just clear the dumb cobwebs out of his brain. Then he could think straight. He felt the bump on his forehead. It was still pretty big and sore.

That weird, squeaky little voice kept ringing in his ears. "Don't flush! Don't flush! Oh, please don't flush!" it had said.

It didn't happen! Pete told himself. There was no *way* it could have happened! Toilets don't talk. Only people talk. And the idea of someone or some*thing* inside the toilet was as weird as a talking toilet.

Pete touched the bump again. Was it possible that he had brain damage?

Pete could hear Mom banging pans in the kitchen as she fixed dinner. Dad was watching the news on

TV. How could they go about their business as if everything were perfectly normal?

What would Mom and Dad do, Pete wondered, when they found out their only son had brain damage? Would they put him in a special hospital?

Pete scooted up on the bed and put his head on the pillow. He had to calm down. Closing his eyes, he took a deep breath. For a moment, he relaxed. Then suddenly he remembered what Bobzee had said— "Dumb old thing threw water all over me." What did he mean by that?

By dinnertime, Pete had made up his mind that he wasn't brain-damaged after all. One thing was clear. The bad plumbing idea was out. Bad plumbing didn't explain the voice he had heard.

There was only one answer. Something was inside the toilet. And that something could talk. Pete decided that before the night was over, he would find out what it was.

Dinner was boring. Pete wasn't hungry. And his parents were driving him up the wall. Dad spent the whole meal talking about responsibility, maturity, and the works. Mom was acting concerned and protective.

"Are you sure you're all right, Pete?" Mom asked over and over. "Maybe you went back to school too soon after your accident."

Dad was right in the middle of his "when I was your age" speech. Then Mom reached over to feel Pete's forehead. "His head feels a little warm, Ed," she said to Dad.

Dad stopped his speech in midsentence. "*That's* not what should be warm," he said.

"But, Ed. It wasn't really Pete's fault," Mom said. "You know how Bobzee is. He's a little—uh—wild."

"He's a little brat," stated Dad. "Which is exactly why he's not allowed inside our house when we're not here." He swallowed the food he was choking on. "That's been a rule around here since that child started walking." He shot a glare at Pete, who was picking at the food on his plate. "Have you forgotten that rule?"

"No, Dad," said Pete. "I shouldn't have let him inside the house. I'm sorry."

Pete wished the meal were over. Then he could escape to his room. He needed time alone to think.

After Pete said he was sorry, Mom dropped the subject. But Dad didn't. "You *should* be sorry," he said. "Your mother and I wouldn't leave you alone if we didn't feel we could trust you to—"

The phone rang. It was the most beautiful sound Pete had ever heard. Especially when the call turned out to be for him. It was Yibbet.

"I'm sorry for my brother's conduct this afternoon," Yibbet said. "During dinner, Bobzee talked about what he'd done at your house."

"How come *you* have to apologize for him?" asked Pete.

"Because he's too young to do it himself," said Yibbet. "Besides, my dad had to go to a meeting. And my mom's busy. So it was up to me."

"Oh," said Pete.

"By the way, Pete," Yibbet said, laughing. "Did you know you have a dragon in your toilet?"

"Huh?" Pete said, almost dropping the phone. "A what?"

"A dragon," Yibbet repeated. "Bobzee said he saw it. He said it was a baby one. So it's probably not dangerous." Still laughing, Yibbet said good-bye and hung up.

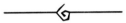

It seemed to Pete he'd been lying on his bed for days. And he was just waiting for Mom and Dad to go to bed.

For the hundredth time, Pete asked himself what Bobzee could have meant by a dragon in the toilet. A bug maybe? A giant-sized bug? One that talked? Oh, sure.

It was after midnight when Pete's parents went to bed. Pete waited ten more minutes. Then he got up and made his way down the hall to the bathroom. He put his ear to the door and listened.

Pete heard water splashing. Through the closed door, the sound was faint. But he definitely heard water splashing.

Pete's hand was trembling when he reached for the doorknob. In his mind, he could hear that funny little squeaking voice again—"Don't flush! Don't flush! Oh, please don't flush!"

Pete's hand dropped to his side. Did he *really* want to open that door? Did he want to know what was in the toilet? A dragon, Bobzee had said. But any fool knew there was no dragon in the toilet. Or anywhere else, for that matter.

The splashing sound was getting louder. Pete's parents' room was just a few feet down the hall. Should he wake them and have them go in with him? He could just hear his dad. "Are you crazy?" his dad would ask.

Pete took a deep breath. He grasped the doorknob firmly. Then, following another deep breath, he opened the door and rushed into the room. He looked into the toilet.

It was there! It was small—not over six inches long. It had fangs and a long tail and scales. It *did* look a little like a dragon. If there were such things as dragons. Except it was *pink*. The pinkest pink Pete had ever seen.

Pete didn't faint. Instead, he stammered, "Wh-wh-who—uh—*what* are you?"

The pink, scaly thing pulled itself out of the water. It rested on the toilet seat. "At the present moment," it said in that same squeaky voice, "I am a crocodile. A very *mean* crocodile."

Pete was shaking from head to foot. But, in spite of that, he giggled.

"What's so funny?" asked the small creature.

"Uh—" Pete started, not knowing how to answer that question. Several things were funny. *Very* funny. Here he was talking to a pink, scaly thing that had just climbed out of the toilet. And the thing had called itself a crocodile.

"What's so funny?" the thing asked again. "Crocodiles are very wild and dangerous. I know all about crocodiles."

"You couldn't know much about them," said Pete. "Or you'd know they aren't pink."

"Oh. Well, what color are they then?" the thing asked.

"I've never actually seen one," Pete said. "But I think they are sort of a greenish-gray color."

"Like this?" the thing asked.

Right before Pete's eyes, the small creature turned from pink to the exact color of a crocodile.

"I guess I was in too big a hurry," the thing said. "But I knew I'd drown if I didn't turn into something fast. A crocodile was the first thing that popped into my mind." He heaved a funny little sigh.

"I was so tired I could hardly see straight," he continued. "That's why I lost my balance. It was such a long way from where I had to land the ship—"

"Ship?" Pete interrupted. "What are you talking about?"

"Why the spacecraft, of course," said the thing. "How do you think I got to Earth?"

Pete was in the middle of a huge gasp when a voice rang out. "Pete, is that you?" hollered Mom. "Are you okay?"

"I'm fine, Mom!" Pete grabbed up the creature and ran down the hall to his room. "Good night!" he called over his shoulder.

Pete shut the bedroom door. He set the thing on the foot of the bed. Now it was a regular-sized gray mouse.

"How did you do that?" Pete asked.

"I'm not sure," the gray mouse answered. "I've never thought much about it. It's just something I have to do when I'm on a mission. For my safety."

"Mission?" asked Pete.

"When I'm sent to other planets," explained the mouse. "When I'm on an assignment. Like now."

"Other planets?" Pete's voice rose. "On an assignment?"

"My, you earthlings are dense, aren't you?" said the mouse.

Pete continued to look dense.

The little gray mouse settled back on its haunches. "I'm a Galunkian," he said. "I live on the planet Galunk." In his squeaky little voice, he went on. "I was sent to Earth to study the earthling ungrowns."

Pete sucked in his breath and sank down on the bed. "*Ungrowns?*"

"Ungrowns," said the gray mouse. "Such as yourself. Small ones."

Pete couldn't keep from grinning. "Ungrowns— that's good," he said. "We're called children—or kids. Or sometimes a lot of other things."

"Well, whenever," said the mouse impatiently.

This time Pete laughed aloud. "I believe you mean *whatever.*"

The little mouse's eyes snapped. "Whatever! Whenever! Whichever! Who cares?" he yelled. "All I know is I got this horrible assignment. And everyone else got to go to the big race."

"What big race?" asked Pete.

"The annual Galunkian spaceship race," said the mouse. "Three times around the planet. And the winner gets the cup. That beautiful, wonderful cup!"

"Sounds super neat," said Pete. "A silver cup?"

The gray mouse giggled. "*Silver!*" he said. "A *silver* cup—that's a good one." Another giggle. "Of course not. The cup is paper. Genuine, 100 percent paper!"

"How come you didn't get to go to the race?" Pete asked.

"Good question," answered the mouse. "*Very* good question. It just so happened that this assignment came at the same time as the race. And I got chosen, naturally."

"*Naturally?*" asked Pete. "What do you mean you got chosen *naturally?*"

"Because of my QI," said the mouse.

"QI?" asked Pete.

"Quotient of Intelligence," said the mouse. He tapped his head with one paw. "Meaning smart. Smart counts for a lot on the planet Galunk."

"I would think it would be a great honor to be chosen," said Pete.

"Oh, it is, it is," the mouse said. "Don't get me wrong." He sighed. "I guess I'm just in a nasty mood. I was disappointed because I had to miss out on the race.

"Plus, I got stuck with the oldest junker on the planet," the mouse continued. "They were using all the best ships for the race.

"I couldn't control it once I got near land. As I said, I had to walk such a long, long way. Then I fell into what must have been an underground river. So I turned into the first thing I found to keep from drowning. I swam around for days. I thought I'd never get out of that—that thing."

"Toilet," said Pete.

"Which—uh—whatever," said the mouse.

"It's really weird how you ended up here," said Pete.

"Weird is not the word," the mouse said. "*Ugh!*"

The mouse stretched. Then he curled up in a tight little ball. "It feels so good to relax—and be dry," he said.

"You must be beat," said Pete. "I know I am."

Pete reached out and lifted the small gray creature onto his pillow. "You can sleep here if you want," he said. "In the morning we'll talk some—"

Pete was interrupted by the opening of his bedroom door. "Who on earth are you talking to?" asked Mom. She was standing in the doorway, looking sleepy and puzzled.

"I-I-I couldn't sleep," Pete stammered. "I was— uh—I was making up a poem for school on Monday."

"At one o'clock?" Mom asked. Suddenly the look on her face changed. "Pete, where did you get that teddy bear?"

"Teddy bear?" Pete asked.

Mom pointed. "On your pillow," she said.

Pete turned. A brown, badly worn teddy bear with one ear missing was lying on his pillow. It was right where Pete had set the mouse.

Pete's mind raced. "Uh-uh-I found it in the bathroom," he said. "I-I guess Bobzee must have left it."

Mom smiled and closed the door.

Pete lay back. He raised himself to his elbow and looked at the teddy bear. The teddy bear grinned. Then it closed its eyes.

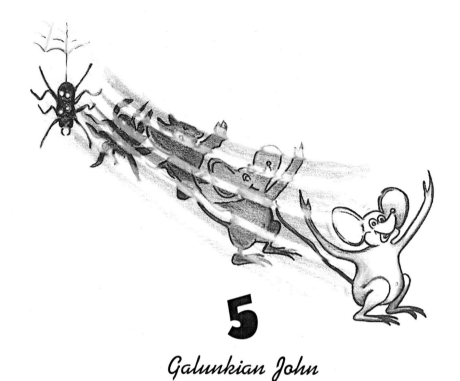

5

Galunkian John

"Hey, Pete, are you going to sleep all day?"

Pete sat up in bed. Through half-closed eyes, he saw his dad standing at the foot of the bed.

"This is the third time I've called you," Dad said. He walked around to the side of the bed. "You okay?"

Pete rubbed his eyes with his fists. "Sure," he said. "I'm fine. Just sleepy, I guess."

Dad walked back to the door. "How did little teddy bear sleep?" he said with a snicker.

Pete felt foolish. He hurriedly crammed the brown bear under the covers.

Pete got dressed and brushed his teeth. He started to the kitchen for breakfast. Then he remembered *it*. But when he turned back the covers, there was nothing there. No bear, no mouse, no crocodile. Nothing!

Pete smoothed out the covers and felt for lumps. "Hey!" he whispered. He looked under the bed. "Where did you go?" He looked inside the closet.

"I'm here," answered a very small voice.

Pete looked toward the sound. All he could see was a cobweb in the corner of the room. "Where?" he asked.

"Right here," said the voice again. The web quivered. And Pete saw the yellow and green polka-dotted spider in the center of it.

"Holy cow!" Pete blurted. "How do you *do* that?"

"I told you before," said the spider. "It just happens. It isn't something I *do*. It's just something I make happen. I think it in my mind and presto!"

"I wish you'd cut it out," said Pete.

"Why?" asked the spider.

Pete shrugged. "Well, it makes me feel dumb," he said. "Talking to spiders and teddy bears—and pink crocodiles. It's not quite so weird talking to a mouse—but a spider!"

The spider laughed. It laughed so hard it fell off the web. But before it hit the floor, it had changed back into a little gray mouse.

"How's that?" it said, looking up at Pete.

When Pete finally made it to the kitchen, he was too late for breakfast. Mom was putting lunch on the table. Pete slipped a slice of cheese and a couple of crackers into his shirt pocket.

"How are you feeling?" Dad asked, seating himself across from Pete.

"Starved," said Pete. "My ankle is all well. And the bump on my head is just about gone. I feel great!"

"You should," said Mom. "You got enough sleep to last you a week. By the way, did you finish your poem?"

"Uh-huh," Pete gulped a bite of food. He took a big swallow of milk. And another. And another. He hoped someone would change the subject before he came up for air.

"How about saying it for us?" Mom said. "I'd like to hear it."

"Naw," said Pete. "It's dumb."

"What's it about?" Dad wanted to know.

"Nothing," replied Pete.

"It's dumb and it's about nothing," said Mom. "Miss Ryan should be wild about it, shouldn't she?"

Pete swallowed the last of his lunch. Then he headed for his room. The gray mouse was nowhere in sight. But the yellow and green spider was clinging to the web in the corner.

"Just playing it safe," said the spider. "In case your mother came in. She may throw a fit at the sight of a mouse."

"Yes, but she'd go nuts at the sight of a spider," said Pete. "Especially one that looks like you." He reached into his shirt pocket. "Hungry?"

"Starving," said the spider.

"I brought you some cheese and crackers," said Pete.

"Spiders don't eat cheese and crackers," said the spider.

"Well, mice do," Pete answered. "And that's what you were when I left."

The spider laughed and turned into a mouse.

Pete watched as the gray mouse sat on the dresser and nibbled the crackers and cheese. When the mouse finished, he shook the crumbs from his whiskers. Then with his tiny pink tongue, he licked his little paws and washed his face.

Pete could hardly hold back his excitement. He had never seen a mouse eat before, let alone wash itself afterward. Even if it was a mouse that wasn't really a mouse at all.

This thought brought a question to Pete's mind. "Say, what do you look like when you're not being a mouse?" he asked. "Or a crocodile? Or a teddy bear? Or a spider?"

"Like a Galunkian, of course," replied the mouse.

"Well, what does a Galunkian look like?" asked Pete.

"Just the way he should," said the mouse.

The mouse continued to wash behind his ears. When he finished, he rubbed his tummy to show how much he had enjoyed the food.

Then the mouse jumped from the dresser to the bed. He motioned for Pete to sit next to him. In a serious tone, he said, "Before we go any further with our relationship, we must get a few things settled."

"Like what?" asked Pete.

"Like do you want to be my sponsor while I'm on this mission?" asked the mouse.

"What does a sponsor have to do?" asked Pete.

"See to my needs," said the mouse. "Be my friend and protect my identity at all costs."

"You mean I can't tell anybody about you?" said Pete.

"Not a soul," the mouse answered.

Pete felt a little let down. He wanted to tell Arthur, at least. But on the other hand, it might be just as well. It was a lot to expect of someone—even Arthur—to keep such a secret. Besides, most people probably wouldn't believe him anyway.

"I promise," Pete said quickly. "I'll never tell a soul. Never."

"Will you take the Galunkian oath?" asked the mouse.

Pete nodded.

"Okay. What's your full name?" the mouse asked.

"Peter Edward Ramsey," Pete replied.

"Okay," said the mouse. "Put your thumbs in your ears, and touch your nose with your tongue."

"I can't touch my nose with my tongue!" yelled Pete in disgust.

"Try," said the mouse.

So Pete tried.

"Now repeat after me," the mouse said. "I, Peter Edward Ramsey, do solemnly swear—"

"Aw, Pee—er—Eb—uh—Am—zee . . ." Pete began. Then he pulled in his tongue and took his thumbs out of his ears. "You're crazy!" he sputtered. "I promise, and that's that!"

Pete was sure the mouse was trying to keep from laughing. And he heard it mutter, "Earthling ungrowns are very quick-tempered."

"There's something else we should settle," Pete said after he'd cooled off some. "I can't keep calling you *Hey*. What's your name?"

"Neila Gnieb," said the mouse. He puffed out his chest. "I was named after my grandfather."

"Oh, I see," Pete said. "It—it's a nice name. But a little long. How about if I call you—" Pete stopped in thought. He remembered where he had found the thing. Pete smiled and said, "John?"

The mouse agreed.

"Okay, John," Pete said. "I have a plan. If I hang around the house, I'm sure to get stuck with a bunch of chores. So here's my idea . . ."

A moment later Pete marched into the kitchen. He was carrying the teddy bear. "I'd better take this teddy bear back to Bobzee before he comes after it," he said.

Mom was caught off guard. She didn't have time to say "Pete, take out the garbage!" or "Have you cleaned your room?" or "Why don't you help Dad wash the windows!"

A block away from the house, the teddy bear became a mouse again. "Hmm," John said as he settled into Pete's shirt pocket. "Ungrowns are very dishonest."

Pete laughed. "The right word is *clever*," he said.

Pete walked to the vacant lot next to Yibbet's house. Yibbet, Arthur, and a couple of other guys were passing a football around.

"Hey, Pete," Arthur called out to his friend. "I called your house twice this morning. Your mother said you were still asleep. On Saturday morning?"

"Come on," yelled Yibbet. She threw the ball to Pete.

The two other guys were from another school across town. One of them, Bill something, was Yibbet's relative. The other, Chuck Ames, was a real jock. If there was one thing Pete didn't want to do, it was to make a fool of himself in front of Chuck Ames. Pete was crazy about sports. But he figured he'd never be more than almost average in sports.

Chuck was backing up across the lot. "Throw it!" he ordered in a booming voice, still running backward.

Pete twirled the football around and around in his hands. He tried to swallow the lump in his throat.

"Well," said John. "Are you going to throw it or not?"

"I can't pass that far," Pete whispered.

"I thought you said ungrowns were clever," said John.

"Clever has nothing to do with passing this ball *that* far," said Pete.

"Hurry up!" yelled Bill. "We haven't got all day!"

Pete drew his arm back. He took a deep breath. And then he heaved the ball with all his might. It sailed through the air, lopsided, and fell at least twenty feet short of Chuck's outstretched hands.

Everyone laughed except Arthur. "He isn't warmed up yet," yelled good old Arthur.

Chuck picked up the football. Pete prayed silently that he'd pass it to someone else. He didn't.

Pete jumped for the ball, but it sailed over his head. It flew over the hedge and into some bushes in Yibbet's yard. Pete went after it. He hoped it was lost. But no such luck.

"Throw it! Throw it!" Chuck was shouting as Pete walked back to the vacant lot.

Again Pete took a deep breath. He drew back and let the football fly. It spiraled higher and higher and over Chuck's head. It flew out of the vacant lot. It went over the house across the street. And it came down in a backyard in the next block.

Five mouths, including Pete's, flew open.

Bill was the first to speak. "Man!" he yelled. "What a pass! He's a regular Joe Montana!"

Pete was still in shock when Chuck got back to the lot. He was carrying the ball under his arm and panting hard. Chuck threw the ball again at Pete, mumbling something about a strong gust of wind.

Pete got ready to jump, sure he would never make it. All of a sudden, the ball stopped in midair, directly over Pete's head. Then it dropped into his hands. Pete squeezed it hard to keep it from falling to the ground.

"Ouch! Take it easy!" The voice, very familiar to Pete by now, was coming from the football. Pete reached into his shirt pocket. It was empty.

"Holy cow!" Pete choked. "I might have known."

Then Pete fell to the ground, rolling and laughing hysterically. The guys stared at him. He didn't stop until Bobzee came running up with a football. "I found the football in the bushes," he said. "And you can't have it back unless I can play too."

When Pete got to his feet, the other football had disappeared. He felt a lump in his shirt pocket. Before anyone could say "How did that football get back in the bushes?" Pete said, "I have to go home. I have chores to do."

"See you later," Arthur called after him.

Arthur arrived later that afternoon. By then, Pete had swept the garage for Dad, dusted for Mom, and cleaned his room. The strange thing was, he really hadn't minded too much. Of course, having John for company helped a lot.

"Ungrowns are helpful," John said when the chores were done.

Pete laughed. "When they want to be," he said.

Arthur helped Pete with the poem. It was no masterpiece. But Pete decided it would satisfy Miss Ryan.

"I am still in awe, Pete," said Arthur. "Your spectacular performance today was totally amazing!"

Pete sighed. "It was something, wasn't it?"

"Chuck claimed it was a freak gust of wind," Arthur said. "Do you think it's possible?"

"I guess we'll never know, will we?" Pete replied.

6

E. T. or Woogo?

Pete hated for the week to end. What a fun weekend he'd had! It was still hard to believe it wasn't all a dream.

He, Peter Edward Ramsey, was an average kid in an average town. And he had been chosen to share a secret with an alien. A being from some planet that no one had ever heard of.

Pete had never actually *seen* the alien being. Not in its true form. All Pete knew was that it could change. Its favorite form so far was a mouse.

Pete felt comfortable with a mouse. It was kind of a neat idea, having a talking mouse. And it was awfully cute.

Pete's big problem was what to do with John while he was in school. He sure couldn't keep him a secret in the classroom. No matter what form he was in.

And Pete was worried about leaving him at home. What if Mom found the spider web in his room? He could just see her whacking it all to pieces with the broom. And crushing the little polka-dotted spider.

Or suppose Mom discovered the mouse. She'd set so many traps in his room. It would be like a mined battlefield.

There was only one thing for Pete to do. He'd have to always get home before Mom.

Pete didn't have to worry much about Dad. Dad always came through the back door. Then he stopped at the refrigerator. Next, he headed for the living room. Then he flopped on the couch until dinner. He practically never went near Pete's room.

But Mom was a clean freak. She was forever running around the house looking for dirt. And Pete's room was the best place to find it.

Protecting his secret would be hard. But it would be worth it. It wasn't every kid who had a visitor from another planet.

Sunday night, Pete took his shower early. Then he got into his pajamas. Next he settled down with a bowl of popcorn. He wanted to watch an old movie on television—*E.T.*

Mom was in the kitchen packing lunches. And Dad was next door helping the neighbor work on his car. It was a good thing they weren't there.

All at once, John the mouse came running across the room. He climbed the couch and settled on Pete's shoulder.

"Are you crazy?" Pete whispered. He shoved the mouse inside his pajama top. "I told you to stay in my room."

"I got lonely," John whispered back. "And something smelled so good. I just had to come and see what it was."

"Popcorn," said Pete. He held the bowl against his chest so John could reach it.

"Mmm—good! Yum-yum!" Pete could hear *crunch*, *crunch*, *crunch* inside his pajama top.

"Ungrowns are generous," Pete heard John say.

"Are you talking to me?" Mom called from the kitchen.

"No, Mom," Pete answered. Then he turned up the sound on the television.

"Hey, keep it down," Pete told John.

Pete leaned back against the couch, watching the movie. John munched away on popcorn.

All of a sudden, John jumped out of Pete's pajamas. He landed on Pete's shoulder. "It's Woogo!" John screeched. "It's Woogo!" He waved a paw in the air. "Hey, Woogo! It's me—Neila Gnieb!"

Pete almost choked on a mouthful of popcorn. He could actually feel his eyes bulging. "Wh—wh—" He slobbered on his chin. "What did you say?"

"It's Woogo," repeated John. "He's from a planet near Galunk."

"But—but how could you know *him*?" Pete asked. His heart was pumping in his chest.

John giggled. "Woogo?" he said. "Everyone knows old Woogo. He's cool."

Pete took a deep breath and tried to calm down. "But you couldn't know him," he explained. "He's not real. He's just a—a made-up character in a movie. He's called 'E.T.' "

John snorted. "Huh! That's what they'd like you to believe," he said. "I guess I ought to know Woogo when I see him." He snorted again. "Not real!"

John crawled back inside Pete's pajamas. "Ungrowns are very trusting," he mumbled.

Pete lost his appetite. He carried the bowl of popcorn into the kitchen. "I think I'll turn in early, Mom," he said.

Mom put her hands on her hips. She looked at Pete with concern. "Are you all right?" she asked.

"I'm fine. Honest," Pete insisted. "I just want to go to bed and—uh—read."

"Instead of watching television?" Mom asked.

"Uh-huh." Pete left before Mom could ask him any more questions.

Pete got in bed and tried to read. But it was no use. His brain was in such a stir.

John the spider had strung up a web in the back of the closet. He had gone to bed early. He claimed he was a little homesick.

It was just as well. Pete wasn't in the mood to talk to John. Not when he wasn't making sense. Woogo? Pete thought. How silly!

Pete turned on his radio and listened to it until he got sleepy. Then he rolled over on his side and pulled the covers over his head.

7

Jesianitaleeann

Pete arrived early at school Monday morning. Samantha was the first person he saw. He forgot that he was supposed to be mad at her. He almost called her name. But then he saw Dwight Phillips running to catch up with her. Together, Dwight and Samantha entered the school building.

Pete kicked the ground as hard as he could. And then he lost his balance. He was flapping his arms around. Just then, a soft voice interrupted his tantrum. "Er—excuse me," said the voice.

Pete froze. His arms were stretched out. His lunch sack was dangling in one hand. He felt like an idiot.

Then Pete saw the girl who had spoken. Her hair was dark. Samantha's was blonde. This girl was tall. Samantha was short. This girl was beautiful. And Samantha was—well—very pretty.

Pete's arms fell to his sides. The boiled egg in his lunch sack crunched as it hit his leg.

"Hi," Pete finally said.

"Excuse me," the girl repeated. "Could you show me where the office is?"

"Sure," Pete said. He could feel other kids watching him as he and the girl walked toward the school building. "You're new, huh?" he asked.

The girl nodded.

"My name's Pete," he offered. "What's your name?" He wished that his voice wouldn't squeak so much.

"My name is Jesianitaleeann," said the new girl.

"Jes—i—an—ita—lee—ann?" Pete asked with another squeak. "Well, would it be okay if I call you Jes, or Jesi?"

The girl frowned. "I'm not fond of nicknames," she said.

"Oh, well. Then Jesianitaleeann it is," Pete said. "It sure is different." But then he added in a hurry, "But pretty—real pretty."

Pete walked down the hall beside Jesianitaleeann. He threw his shoulders back, trying to look taller. But he got a kink in his back.

Pete put his hand on Jesianitaleeann's arm and led her around a corner. "It's down this way," he said.

Just then, Pete came face to face with Samantha and Dwight. Dwight just said "Hi." But Samantha smiled. Not just a little smile—but a *smile*.

Samantha had smiled at him lots of times. Nice smiles, friendly smiles, sweet smiles. Even a disgusted smile. But Samantha had *never* smiled at Pete *this* way.

Pete tried to close his mouth. He knew it was hanging open. But his jaw hinges seemed stuck.

As far as Pete was concerned, Jesianitaleeann and Dwight had disappeared. There was no one else in the hall but Samantha and him. No one else in the world.

Jesianitaleeann was really something, all right. But face it—Pete hardly knew her. He knew Samantha, though. And she was the one who counted.

The bell rang. Pete sighed a big sigh. He let go of Jesianitaleeann's arm. And then he fell in step alongside Samantha.

Pete let his shoulders sag back into place. The kink snapped out of his back. And Samantha wrapped her arm around Pete's as they walked silently to their homeroom class.

School was wonderful that day! Samantha stuck to Pete like glue. He got a *B* on his dopey poem. He beat Arthur fair and square in a wrestling match. Pete didn't know who was the most shocked—Arthur, himself, or the coach.

Pete had an idea about why he was suddenly so strong. He was excited about Samantha's paying attention to him. And his body could barely hold his excitement. So it was probably coming out through his muscles.

Arthur said it was all a matter of controlling one's mind. "You have mastered the power of concentration," Arthur said, shaking Pete's hand. "Because you are not physically strong enough to beat me."

Arthur wasn't being rude. He wasn't being a poor sport. He was simply being honest. Pete didn't care. He was just glad about winning.

Pete ate lunch with Samantha. He secretly looked all around the lunchroom for Jesianitaleeann. But she was nowhere in sight. He hadn't seen her all day. Pete thought she probably went home for lunch.

He felt kind of sorry for Jesianitaleeann. It was hard starting a new school. Especially in the middle of the year. And he was grateful to her. She was the reason

Samantha finally noticed him. Too bad for Dwight Phillips.

It was already the final period. Pete couldn't remember any school day having gone by so fast.

"I'll meet you at your locker," Pete called to Samantha. Then he hurried to his own locker in the opposite direction.

Arthur was waiting there for him. "Want to stay after and shoot some baskets?" he asked.

"Can't," Pete said. "I'm walking Samantha home."

"Instead of playing basketball?" Arthur said.

As Pete walked away, Arthur called, "Now that I think about it, you could have been right. I think you do have a concussion from hitting your head."

Pete laughed and shook a fist at Arthur.

Samantha was waiting in front of her locker, smiling sweetly. As Pete came nearer, her smile turned to an icy glare.

Before Pete could ask what was wrong, a familiar voice behind him said, "Hi, Pete."

Pete whirled about and faced Jesianitaleeann. "I wondered if you'd walk me home?" she asked.

Pete whirled about again to Samantha. But Samantha was already walking out the door.

It took Pete several seconds to get his tongue in place. "Well—I—I . . ." he began.

What could he say?

"Sure, Jesianitaleeann," Pete finally said. "I'd like to walk you home."

Pete and Jesianitaleeann left the building together.

"I live that way," Jesianitaleeann said. She pointed in the direction that Pete lived.

"Me too," Pete said. He threw back his shoulders and winced in silence as he walked along beside her.

No sense in lying. Pete was enjoying every bit of the attention he was getting. But he still wondered where Samantha was this very minute. Somewhere with Dwight, no doubt.

Jesianitaleeann chattered a mile a minute as they walked.

When Pete was able to get a word in, he asked, "Where did you used to live?"

"Oh," Jesianitaleeann giggled. "A place you probably never heard of. A long, long way from here." She giggled again. "I guess you'd call it a hick town."

She sure didn't look like any hick to Pete.

Before Pete realized it, they were in front of his house. "Hey, this is where I live," he said.

With a flip of her head and a smile, Jesianitaleeann skipped up the steps. "Me too," she said.

By the time Pete got to the porch, Jesianitaleeann was nowhere to be seen.

"Hey, watch where you're going," squeaked a voice at his feet. "And close your mouth. You're slobbering on me."

Pete looked down and saw the little gray mouse. He was rolling with laughter all over the porch.

"You!" Pete yelled. "You creep!"

Pete threw his books against the wall. He kicked at the creature. Just in time, the mouse rolled away, laughing harder. "I—was—only helping," the mouse panted. "Looked to me like you needed help."

"Help!" Pete yelled again. "You call that help? Some help! Samantha will probably never speak to me again."

Pete flopped down on the top step. He felt like crying. He couldn't remember ever being so mad.

"Jesianitaleeann," Pete said in disgust. "I should have guessed. What a kooky name."

"I kind of like it," John said. Then he scampered off.

The rest of the day was awful. Pete stayed mad all through dinner.

"Bad day, huh?" Dad asked.

Pete grunted.

Talk about feeling stupid. All the time Pete had thought John was his friend. And look how he'd tricked him.

Later, Pete sneaked John's dinner into his room. There was no mouse or spider or anything else. "Brought your dinner," Pete grumbled. "You want it or not?"

It was several seconds before an answer came. John was under the dresser. "I'm not very hungry," he said.

Pete was sure he heard sniffling. But Pete was still mad. "It's corn bread and apple, if you want it," he said.

There was no answer. So Pete set the paper plate of food on the floor. Then he left the room. As he was closing the door, he heard, "Ungrowns are poor sports."

Yibbet and Arthur picked that evening to drop in with their homework.

"Hi, Pete," said Yibbet. "We thought you'd like to cram for the big test with us."

"Big test?" asked Pete. "What big test?"

"The big test on South America," said Arthur. "The one that Miss Ryan told us about two weeks ago."

"Oh, yeah," Pete remembered. "*That* test. The one that counts for half of our grade."

"That's the one," said Yibbet.

Pete, Arthur, and Yibbet spread their books out on the floor in the family room. They studied for nearly two hours. Pete was having a terrible time thinking. And geography was not one of his better subjects.

Good old Arthur helped Pete while Yibbet studied her maps.

"The capital of Peru is . . . ," said Arthur.

"Bogota," answered Pete.

"No, Lima," said Arthur.

"Oh, yeah—Lima," said Pete.

"The capital of Argentina is . . . ," began Arthur.

"Amazon?" asked Pete.

"No, Pete," sighed Arthur. "It's Buenos Aires. The Amazon is a river."

"Oh. That's right," said Pete.

"North America and South America are connected by . . . ," questioned Arthur.

"The Andes Mountains?" Pete tried.

Yibbet smacked herself on the forehead. "Holy cow!" she said.

But Arthur stayed very calm. "No, Pete," he said. "It's Panama."

"Oh, Panama! Sure," said Pete. "I get them mixed up."

By the time Yibbet and Arthur left, Pete had learned most of the stuff. He was dead tired when he went to bed that night. It had been quite a day.

John was still out of sight. The food was still on the plate.

Pete tossed and turned, unable to go to sleep. Then he heard a buzzing noise in his ear. When he reached out his hand, he touched something soft and warm.

Pete turned on the light and sat up. An adorable little yellow kitten lay curled up in a ball on his pillow. It was purring. Pete couldn't keep from smiling. The little kitten opened one eye and looked at Pete.

Pete laughed out loud and fluffed up the yellow fur. "You turkey!" he said.

The kitten opened both eyes wide. "Turkey!" he exclaimed. "Are you sure? I thought turkeys had feathers. I'm supposed to be a cat. Don't I *look* like a cat?"

Pete wrapped his arm around the kitten. "Never mind," he said. "You just better not be a cat in the morning. Mom's allergic to cats."

Just before Pete dozed off, he heard a purring whisper. "Ungrowns are so nice."

8

Strange Mutts and Purple Ducks

Things went smoothly for a couple of days. John seemed to be trying to make up with Pete.

Pete taught John to work the knobs on the radio. And he showed John his comic books. "It'll give you something to do while I'm away," Pete said.

John was crazy about the comic books. He loved Batman and Wonder Woman and Spiderman. But his favorite was Superman. He was wild about Superman.

In the middle of the night, Pete was awakened by a squeaky, piercing voice. "Up! Up! And awaaay!" This was followed by a crash.

When Pete turned on the light, he saw John the mouse. He had a handkerchief tied around his neck like a cape. And he was lying flat on his back. Right in the middle of broken model airplane pieces.

"My DC-7," Pete groaned. "It's broken."

"So is my back," said John. "But nobody seems to care."

Pete got out of bed and picked up John. He untied the handkerchief from around John's neck. Pete softly rubbed the mouse's back with one finger.

"Better?" Pete asked after a while.

"Better," sighed John.

Pete lay John on the pillow. Then he covered him up with the handkerchief. He picked up the broken model and got back into bed.

"Do me a favor, will you?" Pete said. "From now on, just *look* at the comic books. Don't try to act them out."

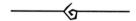

The next day, Arthur wanted to go to Pete's house to do some more studying. He suggested studying in Pete's room.

"It's better in the family room," Pete said. "We can spread our books out on the library table."

"But it's more comfortable in your room," said Arthur. "And we won't be in the way if your parents want to use the family room."

Pete knew it was no use arguing with Arthur. He had a practical reason for every move he made.

Pete didn't really want Arthur in his room. It was hard enough trying to keep John a secret. Several times Pete had almost slipped. If they were in the same room with John, it could be risky.

John wasn't exactly the sharpest mouse—or whatever—in the world, or anywhere else. Chances were, John would do something strange and draw Arthur's attention.

Pete rushed down the hall ahead of Arthur. "Okay, Arthur," he shouted. "We'll go into my room!" He grabbed the doorknob, then paused. "Well, here we are," he shouted some more. "We're going into my room!"

Arthur gave Pete a strange look. Pete felt about the age of Bobzee. In a quiet voice Arthur said, "I hear you, Pete. I hear you quite clearly."

Pete quickly looked around the room. Nothing. Good. At least John was staying out of sight.

Pete had brought cookies from the kitchen. He felt guilty eating in front of John. He bet the little fellow's mouth was watering.

Pete and Arthur studied for about an hour. Then Arthur said, "Let's go down to the Boys' and Girls' Club and swim for a while."

"Good idea," said Pete. "I'll get a couple of towels. You can wear a pair of my swim trunks."

The boys were ready to leave when Arthur paused at the bedroom door. "You know, I don't remember ever seeing a spider quite like that one," he said.

"Huh?" Pete said. "Spider?"

Arthur pointed. "There," he said. "In the web in the corner. It has green and yellow polka dots. I've never seen one quite like it."

"Yeah," Pete said. "It is kind of different, I guess." Pete pushed Arthur out the door. "We'd better get going."

"I'm sure that spider wasn't there when we first went in," said Arthur.

By the time Pete and Arthur had walked one block, Arthur had forgotten the spider. He remembered something else. "Wonder what could have happened to the new girl," he said. "Have you heard anything about her?"

"What new girl?" Pete asked.

"The pretty, tall, dark-haired girl," Arthur said. "The one you seemed to be interested in for a short time."

"Oh—uh—that new girl," replied Pete.

"Funny," mused Arthur. "She was there one day and gone the next."

"Yeah, funny," Pete said. He wished Arthur would change the subject. And Arthur did.

"Whose dog is that?" asked Arthur. "I've never seen him around here before."

Pete didn't have a chance to say "What dog?" or anything else. The strange dog bounded up to him, barking excitedly.

"Hi, fella," Pete said, scratching behind the floppy ears.

The dog licked Pete's hand and barked louder.

"He seems to know you," Arthur said.

"He couldn't," said Pete. "I've never seen him before." To the dog he said, "You'd better go home. Go on now."

The dog didn't agree. No matter how fast the boys ran, the dog kept up with them.

"He—certainly—is fond—of you," panted Arthur.

Pete and Arthur finally reached the pool. The dog was still with them.

"Look, fella," Pete said, squatting beside the brown, slick-haired dog. "You have to go home."

The dog whined and slurped Pete's face.

"He sure is a neat mutt," Pete said. "What breed do you think he is?"

"Just what you said," Arthur replied. "Mutt. One hundred percent mutt."

"He's still a neat dog," said Pete. "Wish I could keep him. Maybe he's a stray."

"Perhaps," said Arthur. "Or perhaps he's wandered away from his home and become lost."

Arthur reached for the heavy door handle. "Are you coming?" he asked.

Pete stood and followed Arthur inside.

Then the dog began to howl—and howl and howl. One of the junior lifeguards walked to the door. "Hey, you stupid beast!" he shouted. "Shut up!"

It worked.

The water felt good to Pete. He made a couple of laps around the pool. Then he lay back in the water, closed his eyes, and relaxed.

"Mmm—nice, huh?" Arthur said, right next to Pete's ear.

"Sure is," murmured Pete. He didn't even bother to open his eyes.

Suddenly, Pete realized there was something wrong with Arthur's voice. When he opened his eyes, he saw that Arthur was clear across the pool. No one was close to him. Just a toy purple duck. And the purple duck was winking at him.

Pete's muscles stiffened. He sunk. He started flailing in the water.

"Hey!" a lifeguard yelled at Pete. "You know the rules of the pool, kid. Get that toy out of there."

Play dumb, Pete told himself when he'd calmed down. After all, he hadn't brought the purple duck in with him. He pretended not to hear the lifeguard.

The lifeguard jumped in the pool and swam toward Pete. "You'll have to get that thing out—" He spun around in the water. "Hey!" shouted the lifeguard. "Where did that purple duck go?"

Pete looked around—and around and around. It was gone!

Pete faced the teenage lifeguard. He couldn't resist a smile. "Purple duck?" he asked. "You saw a purple duck?"

The lifeguard's face turned bright red. He swam away. Fortunately, no one else seemed to have seen the purple duck.

When the boys left the building, the dog was lying under some bushes. When he saw Pete, he jumped up. He bounced over to the boys, panting with joy.

Pete and Arthur began walking home. The dog followed. Near where they'd first seen the dog, they went from door to door looking for its owner. No one had ever seen the dog before.

"You don't think anyone would admit owning that dog, do you?" said one large, bald man.

"You sure that's a dog?" joked a tall, skinny man. "It looks more like a cross between a mule and a penguin."

A lot of people just looked at the dog and laughed. The more fun everyone made of the dog, the more Pete's heart filled with love for it.

By the time the boys had reached Pete's house, Pete was determined to keep the dog. Arthur wished him luck with his parents and left.

Dad got home before Mom that day. Pete was throwing a ball for the dog when Dad pulled into the driveway. Pete gritted his teeth and waited for Dad to laugh.

Dad got out of the car and walked over to Pete. "What in the world do you call that?" he asked, laughing.

Pete told Dad the story. He ended with, "Can I keep him, Dad? Can I, please?" Dad was scratching the dog's stomach. The dog loved it.

"This reminds me of a pooch I had when I was a kid," Dad said.

"Can I keep him? Please?" Pete begged again.

"Okay with me," said Dad. "If we can sell Mom on the idea."

It took a little doing. But between them, Pete and Dad talked Mom into keeping the dog. By the time dinner was over, Pete was the proud owner of a great dog.

After dinner, Pete went to his room. His pockets were filled with food for John.

Pete discovered that John *was* the dog. And somehow, he wasn't the least bit surprised. At least no more surprised than he had been over the purple duck.

In the night, Pete felt something slurp on his face. He woke up.

"Earthling ungrowns are wonderful," said John the dog.

"Yeah, I know," whispered Pete. "So are you." And he fell back asleep.

9

Pooch to Pencil

Pete thought the dog idea was great. A dog was a lot of fun. And now he could bring John out in the open.

Mom didn't think a dog should be sleeping in Pete's bedroom. "It's unsanitary and unhealthy," she claimed.

"It's not unsanitary as long as he's housebroken and he's bathed," Dad said. "And there's nothing unhealthy about it. My pooch slept in the same bed with me when I was a kid. I never caught anything from him. Except maybe a flea bite once in a while."

"Which proves my point," said Mom. "You want a house full of fleas?"

"We'll get him a flea collar," Dad said. "Those things really work."

Dad gave Pete some money. He told him to stop at the store on the way home from school the next day. He could pick up a flea collar and some dog soap.

Mom finally gave in. Pete thought she even kind of liked the dog. Though she said she'd never in her life seen a dog that looked like that.

"Well, who wants a dog that looks like everyone else's?" said Pete.

Mom said she guessed Pete was right.

Pete was really excited about his new pet. Especially when Dad seemed to be enjoying him as much as Pete was.

At the breakfast table, Dad fed most of his toast and bacon to John. He'd break it into little pieces and throw it into the air. John was great at catching things.

"How come you named him John?" asked Dad. "That's an unusual name for a dog. Why not Skip, or Duke, or something like that?"

"Because he's an unusual dog," Pete said. "He needs an unusual name." He ruffled the hair on John's neck. "He's probably the most unusual dog that ever lived."

John followed Pete to school the next morning. He had explained, when they were alone, that he knew the way back home. And he promised to go back home later.

Yibbet and Arthur stopped by the house to walk with Pete. Yibbet liked John. She didn't seem to notice that he was a little different.

"You've got yourself a neat dog there, Pete," Yibbet said.

Pete beamed.

When they were about three blocks from school, Samantha joined them. Well, she actually joined Yibbet. They walked 15 feet behind the boys. Samantha hadn't said a word to Pete since the Jesianitaleeann event.

John ran ahead, sniffing bushes and trees. When he spotted Samantha, he bounded up to her with a welcoming bark. Samantha drew back like she was being attacked by a shark. When she screamed, the dog nearly jumped out of his baggy hide.

Yibbet took over. She told Samantha about the dog. "The poor thing had no home," she said, really laying it on. "No telling how long he'd been roaming the streets. All alone, frightened, and hungry. If it hadn't been for

Pete, no telling *what* would have happened to him. Maybe starved to death or hauled off to the pound and put to *sleep*."

Pete could have hugged Yibbet. Especially when he saw the look on Samantha's face. The four of them walked the rest of the way to school together. Samantha walked next to Pete.

John didn't go back home like he was supposed to. Pete hadn't been at his desk more than ten minutes when he heard John. He was barking and howling loudly at the front of the building.

Pete was angry and embarrassed. All the kids turned around and looked at him. Several kids had talked about the dog earlier. But mostly in a friendly way. John was such a lovable dog. One couldn't help liking him.

Miss Ryan's voice rose above the howling. "We're going to have our test on South—on South America—" she finished even louder.

The louder Miss Ryan yelled, the louder John howled. Finally, she stopped.

"Peter, do you think you could quiet your dog if I let you go out?" Miss Ryan asked.

Pete didn't answer. He just left the room as fast as he could.

"You crazy mutt!" Pete shouted at John. John was jumping all over Pete, licking his ears, chin, and neck.

"Come on," Pete said as he pushed him away. "Knock it off."

"I want to come in," John the dog said in a low voice.

"You can't," Pete said. "I told you. School is not a place for dogs."

"Then I'll keep howling," John said. And he did. Louder than ever.

"Hey—listen!" Pete said angrily. "Just shut up and go home. Or I'll tell everyone who you really are. And where you're from."

John stopped howling. And he stopped being there. He just plain disappeared. Pete batted his eyes and gulped a couple of times. Then he went back to his room.

Pete took a test paper from the room monitor and laid it on his desk. He wondered how in the heck John did that. How did he do any of those things he did? And what did he look like when he wasn't being something weird? When he was a Galunkian?

It sure was hard to keep a secret. Pete wondered if he would ever be able to tell—after John went back to Galunk.

John had told Pete just the night before that his mission was almost over. He had learned what he needed to know. And Pete was really going to miss him.

Pete guessed he'd never really be able to tell anyone. Even after John was gone. Who would believe him? He certainly couldn't prove it.

Pete's thoughts were broken by Miss Ryan. She was standing next to his desk. "Do you intend to take the test with the rest of the class?" she asked. "Or would you like to be excused?"

"N-no, Miss Ryan," Pete answered. And then he looked at the test.

The first two questions were easy because of all that studying Pete had done. The capital of Argentina is Buenos Aires. The capital of Colombia is Bogota.

The third one took some thinking. Name the highest waterfall in the world, which is in Venezuela. Devil Falls, Pete thought finally. He wrote it down.

But—he hadn't written Devil Falls! He had written Angel Falls! Hey, it is Angel Falls, Pete thought. He remembered now. He must have written it without knowing he had.

The next few questions were simple. Brazil produces more coffee than any other country. And the world's largest rain forest is in the Amazon Basin.

Pete gave a pleased sigh. He was doing great. He could feel it in his brain. His eyes darted swiftly around the room. Most of the kids were hunched over their desks deep in thought. All except Arthur. As far as Pete could tell, Arthur was finished. It looked like he was reading a book.

Pete went back to his test. A couple of true or false questions. Some multiple choice questions. Piece of cake, he thought.

Pete's pencil flew. Until he reached the very last question. And wouldn't you know, it was about those two guys—Simón Bolívar and José de San Martín. One was the liberator of the northern part of South America. And one was the liberator of the southern part. For the life of him, Pete couldn't keep them straight.

A quick glance at the clock told Pete he had two minutes left. He racked his brain.

Pete had it! San Martín had liberated the North. He was sure now. But there was something wrong with his dumb pencil. It wouldn't move. It was like he was suddenly losing strength in his hand. Why couldn't he make it write? Maybe he had writer's cramp.

Pete gripped the pencil tightly between his thumb and fingers. Pressing down hard, he wrote José de San Martín in the first blank. But suddenly, the pencil flipped upside down, nearly spraining his wrist. It erased what he had written. And it wrote "Simón Bolívar." Then the pencil wrote "José de San Martín" in the second blank.

Pete dropped his pencil like it was on fire. He stared at it. The pencil rolled into the slot at the top of the desk. He hoped no one in class was looking at him. He knew how stupid he must look with his mouth hanging open.

But whether anyone was looking or not, Pete was not going to talk to a pencil. No way! He had talked to a crocodile, a mouse, a teddy bear, a spider, a football, a kitten, a dog, and almost a purple duck. But he was absolutely *not* going to talk to a pencil!

Miss Ryan said that time was up. She told everyone to bring their papers to her desk.

Pete turned in his paper. He was happy because he had finished the test. And some of the kids hadn't. But he was exhausted. He went back to his desk and slumped down in his seat.

Just wait till he got home, Pete thought. Would he ever tell John what he thought of him! Taking a chance like that!

But John wasn't waiting outside the school.

"Oh, I hope he didn't wander off and get lost," said Samantha. "Or picked up by the dogcatcher."

"I doubt that," said Pete. "He probably just got tired of hanging around and went home. He's pretty smart."

"Pete's right," Arthur agreed. "For a common mutt, he does show a high degree of intelligence."

"Like you, huh, Arthur?" laughed Yibbet.

John wasn't in the yard or the house when Pete got home. At least, John the dog wasn't. But John the mouse was. He was sitting on his haunches in Pete's room eating a cookie.

"I figure I don't eat as much when I'm this size," John said. He chuckled and took another bite. "And to tell you the truth, I'm not too crazy about dog food."

Pete moved closer. He towered over the little gray mouse sitting on Pete's bed. "You're lucky to get any kind of food at all," he said. "After what you pulled today. You deserve to go hungry."

"Pulled?" asked John. "I *pulled* something? What did I pull?"

"Don't play cute with me," said Pete. "You know what I'm talking about. That dumb thing you pulled in the classroom today. A pencil! Holy cow!"

"Dumb!" John cried. "What was dumb about it? I thought you would *like* the help."

"But I didn't need your help," Pete said. "I was doing okay by myself."

"Sure," sneered John. "Devil Falls, huh?"

"You *did* change that!" cried Pete.

"And how about mixing up the names of those two fellows?" asked John.

"I'd have gotten them right," insisted Pete. "Besides, how do you know *you* didn't get them mixed up?"

"You'll see," John said. "You'll see."

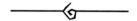

And Monday morning, Pete did see. He got an A+ on the test. Miss Ryan had written "Very Good" across the top of his paper. Not only that, she announced it to the whole class.

"One student got a perfect grade," Miss Ryan said. "That student is . . ." she began. The class all turned to look at Arthur. But when she said Pete's name, the class gasped. Pete thought the gasps were somewhat rude. But so what?

At first break, Arthur told Pete over and over, "I'm proud of you, Pete! I really am!"

"I was sure *you'd* get a perfect grade," said Pete.

Arthur sighed. "So was I," he said. "But I got Bolívar and San Martín mixed up."

Pete put his hand on his friend's shoulder. "Don't feel bad, Arthur," he said. "A lot of people do."

10

Missing John

Pete hadn't cried—really cried—since he was a little kid. But the day finally came that John's mission was over. And he was ready to return to his own planet. Pete broke down and cried hard. So did John.

Pete wrapped his arms around the brown dog's neck. He was grateful that he didn't have to hug a mouse or, worse yet, a spider! Pete sobbed uncontrollably.

John cried dog cries that almost became howls. He slurped Pete's face.

"I'm going to miss you something awful," Pete sniffled.

"M-m-me too," said John.

"Are-are you *sure* you can't stay a little longer?" Pete asked hopefully.

"I-I wish I could," said John. "But I must obey orders."

It was almost midnight. John's spaceship was to blast off in the middle of the night. He hoped he wouldn't be seen.

John would be leaving as a dog. Pete was going with John to see him off. And as a dog, he could protect Pete against danger. Better than a mouse could, anyway.

And if anyone saw Pete, he could say he was looking for his dog. Of course, Pete would have to walk home all alone.

Pete sat on the edge of the bed. He patted John's big, broad head. "I'll always remember you," he said sadly. "But I don't know *how* to remember you. As a dog? Or a mouse? I don't know what you really look like."

"You will," said John. "When we get to the ship."

"Huh?" gasped Pete. "Honest?"

"Honest," John promised. He lay his head on Pete's lap. "Before I leave, I'll show you my Galunkian form."

That made Pete feel a little better. But only a little.

Pete was a little worried that his mom and dad would catch him outside in the middle of the night. But he could say that John had disappeared. And he had gone to look for him. He'd get heck, but it couldn't be helped.

John took one long, last look around the room. He heaved a big, noisy sigh. Then Pete opened the door, and very softly, they walked out.

Before long, they reached the other side of town. John pointed down at the edge of the street.

"Right there is where it all started," John said. "This car came wheeling around the corner. Being a mouse, I thought he was going to run right over me. So I slipped off the curb and fell into that thing. I changed into a crocodile just before I hit the water."

Pete giggled. "You mean you *thought* you were a crocodile," he said. "A pink one at that. Somehow you got into the sewer works. And you ended up in the toilet."

After a while Pete slowed down and looked around. He didn't know how far they'd walked. But it was a lot farther than he'd ever walked before.

Pete noticed that John was several steps ahead of him. So he hurried to catch up with John.

Now they were miles from town. They passed a few darkened farmhouses along the way.

At last, they came to a farm that looked deserted. A FOR SALE sign stood in front of the run-down house. But even the sign looked old. The paint was almost worn off.

"This way," said John. And he took off across a field.

Pete ran to keep up. They passed some old buildings. Then they went through an old orchard. Finally, they came to a haystack that looked like it had been there a hundred years. It smelled like it too.

An old, partly rotted tarp covered half the haystack. But when John pulled the tarp off, he saw more than just hay. It was the spacecraft!

Pete froze in his tracks. He was speechless. He couldn't believe his bulging eyes. He was actually standing beside a spaceship. One that had traveled all the way to Earth from another planet.

Pete was in awe of the ship. Even more so than he'd been of the alien who had shared his room for the past weeks.

Carefully, Pete reached out and touched the spaceship. It felt just the way it should—hard and cold.

John pressed against Pete's leg. "Well, friend, I guess this is it," he said.

"I—I guess so," Pete said. His voice quivered.

"I have to make this as quick as possible," John said. "Those are my orders."

"But wait!" Pete cried. "You said I could see the *real* you. You promised."

"You will," said John. "Turn around and wait until I say okay."

Pete turned around, trembling with excitement.

"Okay," said John.

When Pete turned around, he was face to face with an exact copy of himself. The same face, body, and clothes.

"Hey, come on!" cried Pete. "That's not fair!" He put out his hand expecting to feel the flat surface of a mirror. But he touched a body exactly like his own.

"But—but I don't understand," said Pete.

"Do not try to understand, my Earthling ungrown friend," said John. "Do not question what you see or hear. Accept it for what it is. For what it is, is what it must be."

Pete shook his head. What was going on? This didn't sound like John anymore. His voice was deep and serious. And he was talking strangely.

"Now, my friend," said John, "stand back."

Pete stood back—way back. He stood behind the old mildewed haystack and peeked out.

John pulled open a sliding door and entered the ship. "I'll always remember you," he called out.

Everything happened suddenly. A terrific roar nearly broke Pete's eardrums. A glaring light nearly blinded him. A gust of air knocked him to the ground.

Pete looked up. All he saw was a twinkling, bluish light moving across the sky. He watched until it faded away. Then he started home.

The sun was up when Pete shuffled up the walk to his house. Mom and Dad were both on the porch. Mom was in her bathrobe, and her hair wasn't combed.

"Where have you been?" she cried. "We've been out of our minds."

"We were just getting ready to call the police," Dad added.

Pete's eyes were so swollen from crying that he had to keep blinking to see. "John—John's lost," he sobbed. "I've been looking all over for him."

They took Pete into the house. Mom washed his face. Then Dad led him to his room and tucked him in bed.

"I know how you feel, Pete," Dad said. "Maybe he'll come home by himself. Now you get some sleep. And I'll drive around and look for him."

It was a good thing it was Sunday. Pete didn't wake until dinnertime. He was surprised to find out he was hungry. He thought he'd never want to eat or do anything else again.

But amazingly, Pete felt good—really good. Oh, sure, he'd miss John. He would miss him a lot. But he'd had an amazing adventure. One that probably no other boy in the world would ever have. He'd never be able to tell anyone about it. But he had enough memories to last a lifetime.

"I looked around the neighborhood, Pete," Dad said at dinner. "But no luck. I'll call the pound in the morning and report John missing."

"You know, dear, there's a good chance he'll never come back," Mom said quietly. "Maybe he went back to his home. Or maybe he's just the kind of dog who likes to roam. Who will never belong to anyone."

Pete said he guessed she was right.

"If we don't find him, would you like to go to the pound and pick out another dog?" Dad asked.

"Maybe," Pete said sadly. "Later."

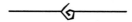

By Monday morning, Pete felt back to normal. He had to keep reminding himself that it had all really happened.

Pete sat down at the table for breakfast. Dad was reading the morning paper and laughing his head off.

"Anything we'd be interested in?" asked Mom.

"Get a load of this," Dad said, still laughing. "Over a dozen people in Lockville reported having seen a UFO. It was going over the town about one o'clock Sunday morning."

Mom sat down and joined in the laughter. "You're kidding," she said. "Right here in our very own town?"

"It takes all kinds," said Dad, laughing harder. "I guess early Sunday morning is when most UFO sightings take place. Wouldn't you say?"

Pete laughed too. Harder than Mom and Dad together.

All of a sudden, Mom let out a shriek. "Look, Pete!" she cried. "There's your dog! He came back!"

Sure enough. A brown, slick-haired dog was sniffing around the garbage can.

For a second, Pete felt dizzy. Then he dropped his books on the floor and tore out the back door.

The dog yipped. He tucked his long tail between his legs and started to run away.

"Hey, boy!" Pete called. He whistled softly.

The dog turned around and slinked back to the boy. Pete patted his big, broad head. When he looked into the droopy eyes, Pete knew at once that this was not John. How two dogs could look so much alike, he would never know. And where on earth had this dog come from?

Mom and Dad joined Pete in the yard. "He looks scared to death," Mom said.

"I guess he thinks he's in trouble," said Dad. Dad knelt beside Pete and rubbed the dog's ears. "Welcome home, John."

Pete turned toward his dad. "I think you're right about his name, Dad," Pete said. "I'm going to call him Duke instead of John."

Because there's only one John, Pete thought to himself. And that's all there ever will be.

PETE RAMSEY AND THE JOHN THING

About the Author

Bonnie Highsmith Taylor is a native Oregonian. She loves camping in the Oregon mountains and watching birds and other wildlife. Writing is Ms. Taylor's first love. But she also enjoys going to plays and concerts, collecting antique dolls, and listening to good music.

If you liked this book, you might enjoy these other Cover-to-Cover titles by Bonnie Highsmith Taylor.

For Honey
Holding the Yellow Rabbit
Tall Shadow